I0717355

ISBN-13: 978-1988083391
ISBN-10: 1988083397

Other books by Shyla Starr:

Persuasive Billionaire BWWM Romance Series

Stacey is trying to keep a handle on her life the best that she can. She is on the verge of losing her job and her apartment, while taking care of her sick grandmother. Her life takes an unexpected turn when she meets Charlie, who works for the construction company that is attempting to persuade her to move out of her home.

Tenacious Billionaire BWWM Romance Series

Adalia is too proud to accept help from the billionaire playboy, Trent Dawson. How long can she maintain her resolve? The bank is at her heels to repossess her business. To make matters worse, Adalia finds suspicious evidence of Trent's philandering ways. She must determine whether to trust Trent with the fate of her business and her heart.

Elusive Billionaire Romance Series

Billionaire Hendrick is trying to repair his company's image by putting in some volunteer work, building a school and hospital for the impoverished children in Africa. There, he meets a beautiful African American volunteer, Jocelyn. They hit it off right away but does she belong in his world?

Lonely Billionaire Romance Series

Tricia was hired to care for billionaire John's wife, who is dying. An unlikely romance emerges after his wife, Rebecca, gives John permission to pursue his happiness after she is gone.

<u>Fervent Billionaire BWWM Romance Series</u>

Alexandra had never been with a white man before. She had seen William at the café before but she always kept her distance. It was unfortunate that their first chance meeting happened when she dropped her breakfast and spilled coffee all over his expensive business suit.

<u>Audacious Billionaire BWWM Romance Series</u>

Chante is torn between staying close to a man beyond her league, and fleeing from him to spare herself from a hopeless position. But she finds she is propelled into a place where she needs to confront her doubts and cast her fate aside to follow the dictates of her heart. Damned if she does and miserable is she doesn't, how will Chante face the events that will lead her to a place of pure happiness or to the pits of a broken heart?

Get the latest update on new releases from the author at:

https://shylastarr.com/newsletter/

This book is Part Two of the "Ardent Billionaire Romance Series"

1 - Love Disrupted

Deirdre doesn't know what to make of the gorgeous man that seems to be interested in her. His name is Parker Walters and he seems friendly enough. There is just something off about him. Why is he trying the hide the fact that he is the heir to his father's billion dollar software empire?

2 - Love Evaded

Deirdre's doubts about her feelings for Felix are brought to light when she unintentionally meets Parker at the Aquarium. Although the chance meeting didn't start off on the best terms, Deirdre finally got the opportunity to present her side of the story. Feeling ashamed and stupid, Parker attempts to make amends with Deirdre, only to be told that she is with Felix now.

3 - Love Requited

Deirdre's luck has changed for the best. Having signed the new recording contract, she was on top to the world. The only thing that could put a damper on it was Felix's attitude. How can he not be happy for her? With billionaire Parker knocking at her door, things are moving off in a different tangent.

Ardent Billionaire Romance Series

Love Evaded

Book Two

By Shyla Starr

Copyright Revelry Publishing 2015

Table of Contents

Chapter One

"**DEIRDRE, I** love that new top." Cassie grinned as Deirdre walked out of the bathroom. It was a Friday night and Deirdre had a date with her new boyfriend, Felix.

"Thanks Cass," Deirdre answered, smoothing the silk fabric of her new peach tunic. The color looked amazing against Deirdre's skin; her plain, black slacks and ballet flats completed the outfit nicely.

"Where is Felix taking you?"

"We're going to try that new Thai place, near the college," Deirdre explained. "Felix has a late class tonight, so I'm meeting him there.

Deirdre had met Felix at the art college where she posed for classes. She'd started by modeling for hobby photographers, but over the last several weeks she'd sat for painters, sketch artists, and sculptors. She'd been offered the job after she'd gone to Simon, the photography instructor, and told him about the teenager at the hibachi restaurant who'd somehow ended up with one of her nude photos.

Simon had been outraged, and had assigned his graduate student Felix to get to the bottom of the situation. Felix had researched everyone in the hobby class, and found that only one had a teenaged son. Simon himself had visited the middle-aged student, and alerted him to the fact that his son was going through his things. The instructor left with all of Deirdre's photos; Felix had gathered photos from the rest of the students, to ensure that Deirdre would never be put in that position again. Simon changed his class policies; only works that didn't depict the model's face could be kept by their creators. Most of the students were sympathetic to the reasons behind the new policy, and many began sketching and painting the faces of their classmates onto Deirdre's body.

After the new policy went into effect, Deirdre happily agreed to pose whenever Simon needed her. On her second trip to the school, Felix asked her out on a date. The graduate student was kind, genuine and thoughtful, and Deirdre hated herself for thinking of Parker Hamlin when she was with him.

A month had passed since the last time she'd seen the gorgeous billionaire, but his face still haunted her thoughts. That morning at his studio, she'd been convinced that he was falling in love with her. She'd already allowed herself to fall in love with him. But then, just as she'd feared, he'd decided that she wasn't the type of person he wanted to be with. Ironically, the job that had brought her to Felix was the same job that had made Parker walk away. Deirdre still wondered what her life would be like now if they hadn't run into that teenager. She sighed out loud.

"What's the matter, Dee?" Cassie asked knowingly.

"Nothing," she replied quickly. Deirdre knew exactly what her best friend would say if she knew that Parker was still in her thoughts.

"Are you sure? You seem distracted… pensive even."

"I'm just stressed about school, Cass," Deirdre assured her. "I feel like I'm never going to finish."

"It'll take as long as it takes, Dee. It doesn't matter when you graduate. It just matters that you keep working at it."

"That's nice of you to say, but it does matter. The sooner I finish school, the sooner I can get a better job and move D'Angelo to a better neighborhood." Thoughts of her brother's safety were always at the forefront of Deirdre's mind.

"You'll feel better next semester," Cassie assured her, "when you're on campus."

Deirdre smiled at the thought of going to real, live lectures as opposed to online classes. She'd managed to land another weekly singing gig that paid better than her Thursdays at Fuseli's. That, combined with her regular modeling sessions at the art college, had made it possible for her to quit her job at the hotel. She'd be able to spend most of the summer home with D'Angelo, and start classes on campus in August.

"Would you have ever thought that my saving grace would come from Carl?" Deirdre laughed. Her ex-boyfriend Carl had been the one who had found her the modeling job.

"Yeah, I bet if he'd known you'd hook-up with Felix, he'd have never set you up in the job." Cassie laughed. "But that's Carl for you. He never thinks things through. I still can't believe what happened to him."

Deirdre nodded. Towards the end of her relationship with Carl, she'd suspected that he was involved with one of the local gangs. After she left him, he'd stopped trying to hide what he was up to. He'd even tried to use her apartment as a stash pad for his illegal activities. Deirdre had refused, and two weeks ago Carl had been arrested for possession of stolen goods and a laundry list of illegal substances. The other gang members were perfectly happy to let Carl take the fall, and word on the street was that he was looking at forty years in a federal penitentiary.

"Maybe he and my mother can reconnect," Deirdre said flatly.

"Have you talked to her recently?" Cassie pressed. Deirdre hardly ever talked about her mother, and talked to her even less.

"I send her pictures of D'Angelo. He used to write letters to send along with them, but he doesn't anymore. She writes once a week… apologizes, says she's changed. She's even found God, apparently. But I don't have anything to say to her."

"Well, we have more important things to think about, don't we?" Cassie smiled. She'd been friends with Deirdre since grade school, and was almost as hurt by Pauline's drug use as her children were. "You need to get going, you don't want to make Felix wait."

Deirdre took one last look in the mirror, kissed D'Angelo goodbye, and rushed out the door.

Deirdre arrived at the small, storefront restaurant and saw Felix's Audi already in the parking lot. She walked through the door and found him sitting at a small, private booth near the back wall. She smiled broadly as she walked over to join him, and he rose to greet her.

"You look beautiful." He smiled as he leaned down and kissed her cheek.

"Thanks," she offered graciously, "how was your class?"

Felix sighed. "It's a freshman level humanities class… no one is there because they want to be, they're there because they have to be. And that includes yours truly." He shrugged.

Deirdre sat across the table, studying her date. Felix was tall and lanky, with blue eyes and curly auburn hair that hung down over his ears. He was attractive in that free-spirited, down-to-earth way. Felix was in his final year of the art college's Masters of Arts program. An artistic genius, he'd attended a progressive liberal arts high school that allowed him to take college art courses. He'd received his bachelor's degree just one year after officially graduating high school; he was on track to finish his master's degree at only twenty-two.

"I'll be teaching what I want to teach soon enough." Felix smiled. "How has your day been? How was D'Angelo's awards assembly?"

Deirdre smiled, surprised that he'd remembered. The last day of school awards assembly at D'Angelo's school had been that morning. Deirdre had mentioned it to Felix only once, and that had been at least two weeks ago.

"It was fantastic." She beamed. "D'Angelo got the Presidential Award for Academic Excellence, and also the Presidential Fitness award. He was the only one in his class who got both. He's ready to make you pay up on his report card too, he has straight A's."

Felix whistled. "And I said ten bucks an A, right? I may have to renegotiate my price for next year or that kid is going to break me," he teased.

Deirdre felt incredibly lucky to have found Felix, if for no other reason than the fact that he was so good with D'Angelo. Felix had lost his own parents in a car accident when he was ten, and afterward his older brother and sister-in-law had raised him. He understood the boy's situation better than Deirdre could ever hope to.

"You could have gotten away with a dollar an A." Deirdre laughed. "But you'll have a hard time convincing him of that now."

"Ah well," Felix conceded, "he's a good kid, and he deserves it. Speaking of which, do you two have plans tomorrow? My seminar was cancelled. I thought maybe we could all do something together."

"That sounds great… in fact, why don't you spend the night with us tonight?" Deirdre suggested. "That way we can get an early start in the morning. D'Angelo has already made a giant list of things he wants to do this summer, you two can negotiate tomorrow's plans over breakfast."

"Are you sure?" Felix asked, a hesitant smile spreading across his face. "I thought you wanted to wait awhile before we spent the night together in front of little man?"

"I'm sure." Deirdre smiled. "He's too young to understand what it means, and he loves having you around. He's been asking me all week if the two of you can have a slumber party."

Felix smiled. "So, I have a fan, huh? That makes me happy… so if I'm having a slumber party with D'Angelo, does that mean I'll be sleeping on the bottom bunk tonight?" he teased.

Deirdre laughed. "We'll see," she answered coyly. They finished their meal in comfortable silence. After Felix paid the check, he followed Deirdre back to her apartment.

"Hey Felix," Cassie smiled when they walked through the door. "If I'd known you were bringing company home I'd have picked up a bit," she said sheepishly to Deirdre.

Deirdre looked around her living room. While she and Felix was enjoying pad thai, Cassie and D'Angelo had erected blanket forts around all of her furniture.

Felix grinned. "Why would you have cleaned this up? It looks like you've just gotten everything perfect."

D'Angelo beamed at the compliment. "Do you like forts, Felix?" he asked eagerly. "We learned all about forts… real ones, in school this year. Did you know there are forts all around the country?" He squealed with excitement. "Dee Dee says if I'm good, we can maybe go visit some over the summer. I want to go to one of the Civil War ones, but Dee Dee says those are too far." He scowled.

Felix nodded knowingly. "They are pretty far… it would take a whole day to drive there. But maybe we can start with the ones closer to home, and work our way out. But that would mean that you'd have to be very good… for a very long time," he warned, taking the conversation as seriously as D'Angelo did.

The boy nodded in agreement. "I can be good for as long as I have to. I want to see those forts," he said with determination.

"Well, I'll do some research, and figure out which one we should visit first. But in the meantime, why

don't we enjoy these fantastic ones you've made?"
Felix suggested, changing the subject.

D'Angelo nodded and he and Felix disappeared
under one of the blankets. Deirdre and Cassie heard the
boy barking orders in his most serious voice, while
Felix responded with a resounding, "Sir, yes sir!"

"You've found a keeper there," Cassie whispered
softly as she and Deirdre moved for the front door. "I'll
get out of here… let you three have some quality family
time."

"He is great with him, isn't he?" Deirdre smiled,
nodding towards the living room.

"Felix is great period, Dee." Cassie smiled as she
walked out the door. "He's a good man. And he may
very well be the best thing that's ever happened to you
and D'Angelo." Deirdre smiled contently as she closed
the door behind her friend.

Chapter Two

'He's a good man,' Deirdre told herself. 'He's a good man… he's good to D'Angelo… he's the best thing that's ever happened to us,' Deirdre told herself over and over again. It was morning; Felix was still asleep, his half-hard cock pressed against Deirdre's hip.

She'd been dreaming of Parker when Felix had rolled over and pulled her towards his growing erection. Startled awake, it had taken her a moment to remember who she was in bed with. Felix's murmuring told her that he was still asleep, but she knew that the moment he woke up he'd be ready for sex. So she laid there, convincing herself to get in the mood. She knew Felix was a good man, a much better man than Parker. She knew that she should WANT to be with Felix. But she also knew that after her vivid dream of making love with Parker, an encounter with Felix could leave her disappointed.

Soft kisses to the back of her neck let Deirdre know that Felix was awake. She moaned lightly in response, willing herself to enjoy the sensations.

"Good morning baby," Felix mumbled softly, slowly moving his growing erection back and forth against her ass.

"Good morning," she breathed lightly, pretending she was just waking up. "What time did you come to bed?" Deirdre had gone to bed early the night before, leaving Felix up with D'Angelo.

"I guess it was around eleven. I'm sorry; I know I shouldn't have let him stay up so late. We were building a Lego village, and I lost track of time."

"That's alright." Deirdre smiled genuinely. "He's out of school… maybe he'll sleep late." She said suggestively, pushing her ass against Felix's cock. 'Cassie was right,' she thought to herself. Felix is the best thing that's ever happened to us.

Deirdre was filled with affection for this beautiful man who was so good to her and her brother. Felix wrapped one arm around her waist and eased his hand under her panties. He massaged her clit with his thumb while two fingers teased her opening. She raised her hip off of the bed and slid her panties off before lifting one leg ever so slightly.

Felix moved under her raised leg and slowly pushed his thick cock into her. He wasn't as long as Parker, but he was certainly ahead in the girth department. Deirdre scolded herself for making the comparison and vowed to push thoughts of Parker from her mind; it was an easy task.

Felix thrust in and out of her slowly, still spooning her from behind. He resumed his light kisses on the back of her neck, and roughly pinched Deirdre's nipples with his soft, artistic fingers.

Deirdre gave in to the sensations that rushed through her body and soon she climaxed in quiet satisfaction. She hadn't cried out, not wanting to wake her brother, but the warm juices that flowed over Felix's balls told him how much she'd enjoyed herself. Content that she was satisfied, Felix increased the speed of his thrusts. To his surprise, Deirdre thrust back against him eagerly instead of collapsing with fatigue.

"Do you want another one baby?" He teased her devilishly.

She responded by squeezing his cock tightly with her firm pussy muscles. Felix cried out loudly.

"Shhh…" she warned him softly, "if you wake up D'Angelo this is over." They each breathed heavily, trying to remain as silent as possible. The harder Deirdre squeezed, the harder Felix had to concentrate on controlling his reaction. When he felt spasms radiating from Deirdre's body, he knew she was close to her second climax. He pounded into her even harder and buried his face into a pillow. His cries were muffled as he emptied his cum deep inside of Deirdre's hot, swollen pussy.

Deirdre's second orgasm left her limp and exhausted. She remained in bed for a while after Felix rose to start breakfast. Finally, when she heard voices from the kitchen, she got up to begin her day. She wrapped herself in her bathrobe before walking towards the kitchen.

She found Felix and D'Angelo sitting at the table, pouring over D'Angelo's summer 'to do' list.

"Good morning," Felix greeted, passing her a cup of coffee. The smell of frying bacon permeated the apartment, and the busted can on the counter told Deirdre that cinnamon rolls were in the oven. "Little man and I have been going over this list," Felix continued, "his summer plans are quite… um… ambitious."

"I know." Deirdre smiled. "I looked it over yesterday. He knows that we won't be able to do all of it," she said, rubbing the top of her brother's head before pulling him in for a hug. "But I told him we'd try… he deserves it, you know… straight A's and everything."

D'Angelo beamed. "That's right Felix, you owe me $80.00."

Felix pulled out his wallet and counted out four twenty dollar bills. "I'm happy to pay up, little man," he said affectionately. "I'm so proud of you." D'Angelo's smiled broadened, and Deirdre was once again hit with a rush of appreciation for her new boyfriend.

"So, what have the two of you planned for the day?" she inquired as she moved to the stove and flipped the bacon.

"Well, it's supposed to do this all day," Felix explained, gesturing to the rain falling outside the kitchen window, "so we were thinking of going to the aquarium."

"They have SHARKS there, Dee Dee!" D'Angelo added with excitement. "All kinds of them… and I bet they have a gift shop!" He squealed, shaking his money in the air.

"Alright, the aquarium it is." Deirdre smiled, pulling the hot cinnamon rolls from the oven. "But first, breakfast."

Chapter Three

"Look at this tank!" D'Angelo called out from across the aquarium. "Look Felix, they have a whole tank of Nemo fish!"

Deirdre and Felix pulled themselves away from the shark tank and joined D'Angelo. Hundreds of clown fish swam through the tank, surrounded by coral and anemones.

"Look!" D'Angelo said, full of excitement. "They live in those weird plant things, just like in the movie… I wonder why they don't have the Dory fish in here?" The little boy pondered seriously.

"I don't know little man, that's a good question," Felix answered. "Before we leave, you should fill out one of those suggestion cards. Maybe the aquarium could do a whole Nemo tank."

Deirdre watched Felix share her brother's excitement and was filled with contentment. She finally seemed to be doing everything right. She was making good money doing things she enjoyed, she had a man that was good to her, and maybe, just maybe, D'Angelo finally had a father figure to look up to.

She was listening to Felix and D'Angelo debate whether or not the sea turtles would be happy in a Nemo tank when her attention was caught by a familiar laugh traveling loudly though the room. Deirdre's stomach turned to knots and her heart filled with dread as she turned in the direction of the sound.

When her eyes met Parker's, she blushed uncontrollably, her body paralyzed by panic. Parker stood at the largest shark tank, flanked on one side by a white haired man Deirdre instantly recognized as Parker Walter Hamlin II. On Parker's other side stood a group of middle-aged Asian men, whom Deirdre assumed were business associates. Parker gave her a cold, hateful glare before turning back to his father. Deirdre forced her attention back to Felix and her brother.

"My goodness boys look what time it is!" she said, trying to sound as cheerful as possible. "The sea lion show starts in five minutes! We'd better go find some seats."

D'Angelo was excited about the show and needed no further encouragement to leave the clown fish tank. They found seats, and for the next twenty minutes Felix and D'Angelo were distracted by the show. Deirdre held Felix's hand and managed to regain her composure before the show ended and the lights came up.

"Dee, I need to go potty," D'Angelo announced as they stood.

"I'll take him," Felix insisted. "I need to go too. Meet you at the sting-rays?" He smiled to Deirdre. She nodded in response and then looked at D'Angelo.

"We've only got two more rooms to go," she reminded him. "You'd better start thinking about where you want to go to lunch."

"I'll think about it Dee Dee," the little boy agreed impatiently, pulling Felix towards the bathroom. "I have to GO!" He danced. Felix allowed himself to be dragged away, and Deirdre made her way to the stingray tank. She stood and watched the oddly shaped creatures glide through the water, silently praying that the Parker Hamlins and their associates had left the aquarium.

"I'm surprised to see you here." A harsh voice startled her from behind. "Admission is a bit steep... I don't want to think about how many photos you had to pose for to be able to afford it." He sneered condescendingly.

His words filled Deirdre with fury, and she turned to face him. "For your information, the aquarium offers a discount if you show them your university I.D." She pulled her faculty badge and her student I.D. card from her purse and shoved them in his face. "Not that there's any reason to explain myself to you," she snapped. Parker studied her I.D.s before shoving her hand away from his face.

"So, what faculty task are you performing exactly?" he retorted. "Last I heard, the university didn't have a pornography department. Do your bosses know that you take your clothes off for money?"

"Again, I don't have any reason to explain myself to you," Deirdre spat. "But if you must know, my bosses are completely aware that I pose in the nude. I'm posing IN THEIR CLASSROOMS. Which you would know, if you'd bothered to let me explain myself at that damn hibachi place. But no, you didn't want to hear it. If you'd given a damn about me at all, you'd have at least let me talk. But you didn't want to hear it, did you? YOU deserved a chance to explain yourself when you fucked up, but I didn't even do anything WRONG!" she cried out loudly.

"Deirdre…" Parker tried to respond, but Deirdre was on a roll.

"No," she said firmly. "You don't get to talk. It's my turn now… I was right all along," she continued, "once you found out who I really was, what kind of family I came from, you started looking for your way out. And that snot-nosed little bastard handed it right to you." She finished spitefully. From the corner of her eye, Deirdre saw Felix and D'Angelo enter the exhibit room. She fiercely stared Parker down for another moment before speaking again.

"If you were a better man, you'd have taken the out I offered instead of blowing that picture out of proportion. Now if you'll excuse me, I have two very important men waiting for me." She turned and walked quickly over to the large eel tank that had grabbed D'Angelo's attention.

"Is that Parker?" D'Angelo asked curiously. "Do you have another school job to work on?" Felix shot her a questioning look.

"Yes, that was Parker." She sighed. "But we won't be working on anymore school jobs together," she explained. "Parker and I don't have classes together anymore."

"Are you alright?" Felix asked, his voice full of concern.

"I'm great," Deirdre smiled, winding her arm through his, "just hungry. Have you two decided where we're going to lunch?" She half listened to D'Angelo's answer as she watched Parker Hamlin disappear from her life once more.

<<<>>>

"Dee…" Steve hesitated "… I have… he sent…" Steve stumbled over his words. He held up a martini and tilted his head towards the other end of the bar. "Parker is here. He asked me to bring this to you, and tell you that he wants to talk."

A hostile look spread over Deirdre's face. "You can tell him…" she started.

"I know, I know," Steve interrupted her quickly. "I told him you don't want to see him. I told him you're happy, and that if I had anything to say about it he'd never be allowed in here again. But his dad has pull, and Fuseli refuses to ban him from the club."

"I know," Deirdre said, "but if this shit doesn't stop I'm going to ban myself from the club." This was the second Thursday since that day at the aquarium, and it was the second time Parker had shown up for her performance. Last week, Deirdre had spotted him in the audience and snuck out the back door the moment her show was over. He must have hidden himself better this week, because Deirdre hadn't spotted him from the stage.

"Now don't go doing anything rash, Dee," Steve advised her. "Just keep ignoring him, if he has any self-respect at all he'll get the point and leave you alone."

"I hope so." She sighed. "I'll see you next week Steve." She rose, gathered her things, and rushed out of the club. She'd almost made it to her car when Parker called out after her.

"Deirdre, please," he shouted. She continued walking, refusing to acknowledge his presence. Parker picked up his pace, and made it to Deirdre just as she was about to open her car door. "You were right, okay?" he shouted again, struggling to catch his breath.

"I know I was right, you didn't have to chase me down to tell me," she said hotly.

"You were right…" he said again "and I was wrong. I saw that picture and the first thing I thought of was my father."

"So, when you looked at a nude photo of me your mind immediately went to your dad?" She laughed mockingly. "It sounds like you have a serious, fucked up problem. You should be talking to a therapist, not to me."

"Deirdre, that's not how I meant that and you know it. That kid pulled out that picture, and I panicked. My father has very strict ideas about what's acceptable behavior and what's not. And I jumped to conclusions. I assumed that you'd posed for some trashy magazine, and that my dad was sure to find out about it eventually. The press can be brutal, Deirdre, and I knew that the second we went public they'd start digging up dirt on you. It's how they operate… and with a picture like that floating around, things are bound to get ugly. I could just hear the lectures… the demands that I break up with you. I did what I did, because I thought it was the best solution for everyone. But I was wrong… I was so wrong. And I miss you," he added softly.

"That's your problem," Deirdre answered shortly. "You've missed your chance. I've met someone… someone who's good to me, and to D'Angelo… takes him for ice cream when he says he will…"

"I know. I saw what was going on at the aquarium. And I'm sorry I disappointed D'Angelo and didn't take him for dessert after dinner that night. But I want a second chance, with both of you," he pleaded. "This new guy, he's good to you. But can you honestly say you feel more of a connection to him than to me? I meant it when I told you that morning I've never felt this way before, and I believe you meant it too. Look me in the eyes and tell me that you're more attracted to him, that you feel more for him than me, and I'll walk away right now," he said, leaning in close to Deirdre, searching her eyes for a response.

"I do… he doesn't…" Deirdre stumbled. "What I do or do not feel is none of your business," she finally answered.

A glint of hope flashed across Parker's face. "I think it is my business, but I won't argue with you right now. We both know I'm right. And I don't care what I have to do, or how long it takes, I'm going to prove myself to you Deirdre. I'm going to show you how much I want you and D'Angelo in my life."

Deirdre studied him as he talked; his words stirred her heart while his appearance aroused her body. She was ashamed of the reaction.

"I have to go," she said quickly, breaking eye contact with Parker. "Cassie is home with D'Angelo. I told her I wouldn't be late. I obviously can't stop you from showing up, but I'm telling you, you're wasting your time. You've proven that we won't work, we're too different. Nothing that you could say or do will change the fact that we come from opposite places."

Parker moved out of her way and allowed her to get into her car. He smiled as he watched her pull away, confident that he'd win her back soon enough.

Chapter Four

"That pompous ASS!" Cassie shouted through a mouthful of French toast. She swallowed before speaking again. "I can't believe he thought he could just swoop in and steal you away from Felix. Does he think that because he's a bazillionaire, he's just entitled to everything and everyone he wants?"

Deirdre nodded silently while chewing a piece of bacon. "It was weird though… he apologized… he admitted he was wrong. He seemed sincere… and strangely confident."

"Cocky you mean, not confident," Cassie interrupted her. "He shows up, spouts off a bunch of bullshit about magical feelings and expects you to drop everything and jump on his cock. That makes him COCKY."

"I know, I know," Deirdre said quickly, trying to avoid another lecture from Cassie; she'd already received three since she'd come home the night before.

"I'm telling you, Deirdre, you should have thrown that damn drink in his face. Or his lap… I still can't believe you talked to him!"

"He… he wasn't wrong." Deirdre blushed. Her friend studied her for several moments before responding.

"He has you hooked, doesn't he? You've bought into the magical feelings bullshit. You've drank the fucking Kool-Aid. How many times does he have to treat you like shit before you stop listening to him? This is just like Carl." Cassie scowled with frustration.

"This is NOTHING like Carl," Deirdre answered defensively. "First of all, Parker isn't a criminal… he wasn't raised around criminals, and I highly doubt he'd ever get me shot at."

"No… but…"

"But nothing. I'll be the first to admit that Parker has acted like an ass, but he always catches himself, he apologizes. And the things he said… about never feeling like this before… I really DO feel the same way, Cass."

"…. What about Felix?" Cassie asked softly. "Remember him? The guy who calls when he says he'll call, shows up when he says he will, takes care of YOUR BROTHER."

"Shhh…" Deirdre warned. D'Angelo was still asleep and she wanted to keep it that way for as long as possible. "I know, I feel like shit Cassie! I don't WANT to have feelings for Parker. I want to have these feelings for Felix. I've been trying to… convincing myself that I really do. And then Parker shows back up and Felix feels more like a good friend."

"Yeah, Dee and Parker knows that. Why do you think he keeps showing back up?"

"I don't know, the Aquarium was a coincidence. There's no way he could have known I was there. We didn't decide to go until that morning."

"Showing up at the club isn't a coincidence," Cassie reminded her. "That man knows what he's doing. And Felix deserves…"

Deirdre interrupted, "What, Cassie? A girlfriend who's hung up on another man? Someone who doesn't love him the way he loves her?"

Cassie pondered the question for a while. "Are you sure that you'll never love him back?"

"No," Deirdre admitted.

"Well then, just give it time. You're allowed to take time when you're not sure about someone."

"And if Parker shows up again?"

Cassie sighed. "I guess you're giving that time too. One way or another, this will work out the way it's meant to."

Deirdre sighed, wishing she shared her friend's faith.

"Ms. Clarke?"

Deirdre turned to find a beautiful, well-dressed blonde woman approaching her.

"Brooke Hightower," the woman greeted her with an extended hand "I'm with Heart Records, and I was wondering if I could have a few moments of your time?"

"Of course," Deirdre stumbled over her words, "it's so nice to meet you." She led Brooke to a small table and took a deep breath, determined to act like a professional.

"Well, I have to say Ms. Clarke, I can't remember the last time I had to hunt so hard to find someone. I caught one of your shows at Fuseli's about a month ago, but you disappeared before I had a chance to speak with you. I stopped there a couple more times, and Steve told me last night that I could find you here."

Deirdre blushed, surprised by the effort the woman had made to find her. "I had a conflict in my schedule… family obligations… so I won't be performing at Fuseli's for a while," she explained.

Brooke nodded. "This place is a better fit for you anyway," she said, gesturing around the bar. 12 East End was modeled after an old-fashioned speakeasy, and Deirdre's voice matched the atmosphere perfectly. Word had already spread that East End had a fantastic new headliner on Friday nights, and the place was packed to capacity.

"Let me get straight to the reason I'm here. I'm prepared to offer you a recording contract. You'll have to record a demo first, and audition for some of my colleagues. But don't worry, those are just formalities. Once the other people in my office hear you sing, I am confident that I'll be able to get you a premium contract… big advance, high sales percentage, even complete creative control, if you want it." Brooke smiled.

Deirdre sat stunned. She couldn't believe what she was hearing, what she was being offered. "I'm sorry," she finally spoke, "but are you sure you have the right person?"

Brooke smiled. "He said you have trouble believing good things can happen."

"He… you mean Parker," Deirdre said softly, realization setting in. "He sent you."

"Quite the contrary actually. He said I shouldn't bother. Parker and I saw you together at Fuseli's after dinner one night. I tutored him in high-school, not that we went to the SAME high-school, mind you. Anyway, the moment I heard you sing I knew I had to sign you." Brooke pushed a manila envelope across the table.

"Here's a mockup of the contract I intend to offer you. There're also three years of financial information on the company and a list of our current artists. By all means, do your own research if you'd like. Whatever it takes to convince you that this is for real…"

Deirdre didn't know what to think. She'd never even dreamed that something like this would ever happen to her, and she didn't know how to respond.

"My contact information is also in the packet," Brooke said kindly. "You take some time, think things over, talk it out with your family. If you decide that this is something you'd like to pursue, give me a call and we'll schedule the recording session for your demo."

"Thank you." Deirdre smiled, finally finding her voice. Brooke nodded as she gathered her things and then disappeared through the front door of the bar.

I'm going to talk it over with someone all right, Deirdre thought grimly. She rushed to her dressing room, changed clothes, and then set off to find Parker Hamlin.

A wide smile spread across Parker's face when he opened the door and discovered Deirdre on the other side.

"Good, you're here," she said sharply, pushing past him into the studio.

"I wanted to be where you could find me," Parker admitted sheepishly.

"So, you do know then? Did you send her? Did you PAY her?" Deirdre demanded.

"Deirdre, I don't know what you're talking about. I HOPED you'd want to find me, so I've been staying here every night… Her who?"

"Your leggy blonde tutor," Deirdre snapped. "Don't pretend you don't know. This whole situation has you written all over it. One minute I'm singing at a local bar, the next I'm being offered a recording contract?"

"Ahh…" Parker sighed. "Brooke. She got to you then. I knew you'd react this way, this is exactly why I told her to leave you alone."

"I don't believe you," Deirdre said harshly. "I think you're trying to buy me. You fucked up, and now I'm with someone else. And you can't stand it. Suddenly, I'm good enough for you again. And what better way to win out over Felix than to give me something he can't compete with."

"I've told you, I had nothing to do with Brooke's offer. I know you Deirdre, and I know that you can't be bought. And for the record, I'm confident that there are many things I can give you that your boyfriend can't compete with… And none of them have to do with money or record deals." As he spoke, he walked towards Deirdre. She backed away as he approached, and she was now up against the wall with Parker pressed against her. She felt his erection press against her thigh as he whispered into her ear.

"I've missed you…" he murmured softly, teasing Deirdre's neck with his breath. "Can you honestly say you haven't missed me?" He kissed her neck softly and Deirdre struggled to pull away.

"It's your own fault you miss me, you're the one who ended things," Deirdre reminded him. This time her voice was filled with regret instead of hatred.

"I know that," Parker answered, pushing her back into the wall. "I regret driving away from you that day more than anything else I've ever done."

A thought Deirdre had had earlier popped back into her mind, and she shoved Parker away.

"Brooke... have you ever..."

Parker laughed. "With Brooke? No. But I'll admit, it's not from lack of trying on my part. She turned me down for two years before I gave up. We've been close friends ever since. We have similar tastes. Her wife looks a lot like you." He laughed again.

"I have to say, I'm happy that the question was bothering you," he continued. "Obviously, you still have feelings for me."

"That's not..."

"Yes it is," Parker interrupted. "You have feelings for me. I have feelings for you. When are you going to stop fighting it?"

Deirdre opened her mouth to protest again, but before she could get a word out Parker wrapped one arm around her waist, pulled her close, and forced his mouth onto hers. Deirdre fought him for a moment before giving in to her desire. Her tongue searched Parker's mouth as his hands explored her breasts. In one swift motion, Parker lifted Deirdre off of the ground and she wrapped her legs around his waist. He backed her up to the wall again, this time to help support their weight. Just as Parker reached up her skirt and pushed her panties to one side, Deirdre remembered Felix. Sweet, reliable Felix was waiting at home for her with D'Angelo.

"Stop. Stop it," she said sharply, putting her feet back on the ground. "I'm with someone. Regardless of how I may feel for you, I'm not a cheater. And Felix is a good man. I may even love him… I won't hurt him like this."

To Deirdre's great surprise, Parker agreed with her. "You're absolutely right, I'm sorry," he said, backing away from her. "When this happens… and it will happen, Deirdre… I want it to mean that we're back together… for good."

"Those are lofty ambitions, Parker," Deirdre teased. "You sound a little cocky even."

"It's not cockiness," Parker said sincerely. "It's faith. I have faith in us, and I know that one day we'll be together again. And I'm willing to wait as long as it takes."

-To be continued in Book 3-

If you enjoyed this title, I would appreciate your leaving a review of the book. Good reviews encourage an author to write as well as help books to sell. Good reviews can be just a few short sentences describing what you liked about the book without having a spoiler. If you could spend 30 seconds writing a review, I would appreciate it: you can review this title right now at your favorite retailer.

Here is a preview of the **next story** you may enjoy:

Loved Requited - Ardent Billionaire Romance Series, Book 3

"**I'M SO** proud of you Deirdre. Here's to a successful demo recording." Cassie smiled. Deirdre lifted her glass of champagne to her friend's toast.

"Brooke said it went really well," Deirdre told her friend. "She said we can expect a decision from the studio execs in the next week or so." Deirdre had spent all day recording what could turn into her first album. She'd been working for weeks, choosing songs that were perfectly suited for her strong soprano voice. This after recording dinner with Cassie was the first time she'd allowed herself to relax in six weeks.

"I just know they're going to sign you. You deserve something fantastic like this, Dee." Cassie smiled. "And just think of all of the things you'll be able to do for D'Angelo. You're going to be able to give him an amazing life."

An uncomfortable look spread across Deirdre's face. "Do you really think so? Felix is afraid that if I'm in the public eye, D'Angelo will suffer for it… I'm afraid he has a point. I mean, look at how most celebrity kids turn out. It's ridiculous… I'd never want that for my brother. I loved recording the demo, but maybe this isn't something I should pursue. Maybe I should just keep focusing on school and let D'Angelo have a quiet life." Deirdre sighed.

Cassie took a long sip of her champagne and studied her friend. "Do you really think that a little attention and money will be worse for D'Angelo than what he's already been through?" she asked firmly. Deirdre opened her mouth to respond, but Cassie kept plowing on. "He deserves the best, even more than you do. And you're a good person, Dee. You'll make sure he is too." She paused for another moment before continuing. "This doesn't sound like you, Deirdre. Whose idea was it for you to turn down the deal?"

Deirdre looked down before answering. "Felix just pointed out that fame can be fleeting. And leave lasting damage. I just don't know what the right thing is…"

"And Parker? I'm assuming you're still talking to him?" Cassie prodded.

Deirdre shook her head. "He's been keeping his distance. He sent flowers once… he's sent over food with notes, saying he's thinking about me, knows I'm busy. And he's been taking D'Angelo to ball games… but he always stays in the hallway… like he's literally giving me my space. He said he'd wait as long as it takes, I'm starting to think he meant it."

"Maybe I misjudged our handsome billionaire," Cassie conceded. "And maybe you should talk to him about your decision. Who would know better about the pros and cons of having enormous loads of money?" She laughed.

"I'd love to talk to him about this," Deirdre agreed, "but I'm not sure I can trust myself around Parker. The last time we were alone together, I almost cheated on Felix. He doesn't deserve that."

"Deirdre, it almost sounds like you're staying with Felix out of obligation. Aren't you the one who pointed out that he deserves better than that?" Cassie reminded her.

Deirdre sighed. "And aren't you the one who said I was allowed to take time?" She countered.

"Yes… but that was back when Felix seemed like a good fit for you. The longer you've stayed with him, the less I think that. He's discouraging you from taking advantage of a once in a lifetime opportunity… It almost sounds like he's intimidated by the idea of you succeeding."

"Felix loves D'Angelo,'" Deirdre snapped defensively. "He's just trying to make sure I put his needs first, that's all. You should see the two of them together, Cass. D'Angelo loves him. And Felix has a point; my decisions affect my brother as much as they affect me."

"It sounds like Felix wants you to put HIS needs first and he's hiding behind an eight year old," Cassie said firmly. She sighed. "We've gotten off track, Dee, tonight was supposed to be a celebration. Take the deal or don't take the deal, it doesn't change the fact that this is a pretty big honor. I'm proud of you." Cassie smiled.

"It is kinda a big honor, isn't it?" Deirdre smiled, allowing her friend to change the subject.

Cassie nodded. "And it could be the beginning of the rest of your life."

<<◇>>

Deirdre slowly unlocked her front door and gently pushed it open. She crept into the living room and found D'Angelo and Felix asleep on the couch, the menu screen of The Lion King shining from the television set. Deirdre kneeled down and shook Felix slightly.

"Hmm," he murmured, opening his eyes. "What time is it?"

"It's a little after eleven," Deirdre whispered. "Cassie and I didn't stay out long. I was ready to get home." She smiled, moving to D'Angelo's side of the couch. She leaned down and kissed him lightly all over the face. D'Angelo woke up laughing.

"How did the song making go Dee Dee?" he asked with bright eyes and a tired smile.

"The song making went great little man." She smiled. "I'll make you a deal. Go to your room and go back to sleep, and as soon as you wake up in the morning I'll tell you all about it."

"You promise?"

"Absolutely," Deirdre assured him. D'Angelo jumped up, hugged his sister and Felix, and then scampered off to his bed.

"He's such a good kid." Felix smiled. "So, it really went well?"

"It really did." Deirdre smiled. "But I'm still thinking about what you said. I'm not sure that kind of lifestyle is best for D'Angelo."

"Well, whether you accept a contract or not, this is a great honor Deirdre, you should be proud of yourself. I'm proud of you." He grinned.

Deirdre sat on Felix's lap, leaned over, and lightly nibbled his earlobe. "Wanna show me how proud?" she whispered suggestively.

"Always…" he said quickly before covering her mouth with his. Felix wrapped Deirdre's legs around his hips, stood, and carried her into the bedroom. He fell backward onto the bed, pulling away from Deirdre just long enough to pull her shirt over her head. Deirdre unhooked her bra and threw it aside and then shimmied out of her slacks. Felix took her right breast into his mouth roughly, biting and pinching her nipple until Deirdre burned with desire.

"Hey Felix, I've had a long day," Deirdre breathed heavily. "Would you care to take this to the shower?" She grinned mischievously.

"Always." he said again, returning her grin. Deirdre climbed off of Felix and shook her ass as she walked to her bathroom. Felix jumped from the bed, stripping off his clothes as he followed.

If you enjoyed this sample then look for **Loved Requited - Ardent Billionaire Romance Series, Book 3.**

Here is a preview of **another book** you may also enjoy:

Love Bound - Lonely Billionaire Romance Series, Book 2

TRICIA SAT in her childhood home and gazed at the wall; today had been particularly trying. In addition to flying from Seattle to Dallas, she had immediately started to take care of her mother. Diagnosed with Alzheimer's, her mother also had a heart condition, and like always, had refused to take any medicine.

Before she had moved to Texas, her mother had lived in Alabama where she saw the effects of the Tuskegee Experiment that lasted long after the experiment had officially ended. African-American men who were diagnosed with syphilis in the 1930s were tracked for forty years to see the long-term effects of the disease. Even when a cure came out in the 1950s, the doctors had not cured the men. Instead, they told patients who wanted to be treated that they had already been given medicine. Hundreds and thousands of people from the families were infected and affected by the trial.

Due to this, Tricia's mother refused to listen to white doctors. The crotchety old woman refused to believe that medicine would help or that anything was wrong with her. After an hour of trying and failing to convince her mother to take the medicine, Tricia had finally given up. She had made some bread pudding with dinner and sprinkled crumbled tablets into her mother's portions. It may not have been the most honest solution, but it worked. Now, Tricia was just exhausted.

Moving back to the kitchen, she started to make herself a cup of chamomile tea. With her mother in bed, it was time to drink some tea and unwind. Thankfully, she only had another two days until the weekend. Her brother Tyrone had promised to take care of her mother over the weekend so that Tricia could take a break and catch up with some old friends.

Sipping her cup of tea, she went to the bathroom and turned on the bathwater. As bubbles and warm water filled the tub, she slowly began to remove her clothes. Only a few days ago, she had left John. After telling him of her decision to return home to her mother, she had not talked to him or seen him again. Their brief fling had been as passionate as it was short-lived. She had taken care of his wife during the final stages of ALS.

Although they had tried to stop their sexual desires from taking over, John and Tricia had made love more than a couple of times. It was wrong and she still felt guilty. Despite her ethical concerns, she found herself wishing that she was still with him. His confident nature and unwavering conscience had attracted her to him from the moment they met.

Easing herself into the water, Tricia laughed to herself. If only her mother knew that she had slept with a rich, white man. She would never forgive her. Tricia picked up Jane Eyre and tried to read, but even her favorite novel could not distract her mind. She wanted John more than anything. It was impossible for her to go without sex anymore. After realizing how fulfilling and satisfying sex could be with him, she was not willing to go back to her normal celibate lifestyle.

She glanced at the bathroom door and saw that it was locked. Moving her hand down her body, she closed her eyes and pretended that her hand was John's. Tricia ran her fingertips around the dark cocoa-colored skin around her nipples and then drew it down further. Initially, she started playing with the soft lips around her clit. This was not enough to satisfy her for long. She moved her clit in slow circles as she imagined John entering her for the first time in the office. The sex had been so magnetic, so electrically charged. She imagined his hard muscles moving against her and moaned.

The moan startled her. She looked at the door to see if her mother had heard anything. There were no sounds from the rest of the house. Moving her hand down along her body again, she moved her fingers faster and faster. Tricia could feel herself approaching orgasm when a sudden sound surprised her. The shrill ringing of the phone pierced the air.

For a moment, Tricia thought about ignoring it and finishing herself off. With a belabored sigh, she stood up and grabbed a towel. It could be someone important for her mother.

Exiting the bathroom, she rushed to reach the phone before it stopped ringing. "Hello?" she said with a breathy voice…

If you enjoyed this sample then look for **Love Bound - Lonely Billionaire Romance Series, Book 2.**

Here is a preview of **another book** you may also enjoy:

Love Astray: Audacious Billionaire BWWM Romance Series, Book 2

"**ARE WE** doing spring cleaning?" Markey Green asked his sister Chante as he eyed the clothes strewn all over her bedroom floor.

"What? No…no…no…" Chante replied, as she pulled another hanger from inside her clothes drawer.

"I just need to find the right one…" she added as she positioned the dress in front of her and stared at her reflection in the mirror.

She shook her head in disapproval. "Too revealing," she muttered under her breathe.

Markey advanced slowly into his sister's bedroom. He didn't want his wheelchair to run into the dresses that were piled haphazardly on the floor.

"Must be a hot date then," he smiled with amusement as his sister began to attack the shelves where her shoes rested.

Chante stopped momentarily. She was surprised at her brother's spontaneous perception. She smiled trying to mask the concern in her eyes. He had grown so much thinner these last few months. His ALS had progressed so much faster than she thought.

"And what do you know about having a hot date, hmmm…" she said as she tousled his hair.

"Well…enough to notice that you're excited once again. These last few months you just seemed… sad." Markey replied.

Chante felt a twinge of guilt. She honestly didn't realize her brother noticed at all.

"Was I that bad…" she asked as she sat down on the bed.

"Bad? Nah, you were just sad." Markey answered wryly.

"Yeah, I guess I was…but I'm ok now…so don't you worry about me kid." Chante replied.

She never told him about the way she felt. In fact she hasn't told anyone about it. Who would believe her anyway? It isn't everyday that a good-looking and wealthy... very wealthy... Jared Lowell asked you to be his sex toy.

Chante tried to forget everything that happened that day on the roof deck of NY General Hospital. She remembered him calling her name as she pushed the metal doors aside and ran towards the freight elevator. She punched the button on the lift and went all the way to the basement where she knew she would be safe. She was confused, her mind was in a whirl, and she wanted to stay away from prying eyes. She stopped by a wall and there amidst rows of empty cars she slumped down on the hard cement floor as despair and disillusionment brought waves of tears that shook her to the core.

"How dare him…" she muttered disconsolately, "he must think I'm scum."

Jared Lowell, heir to the fortunes of Lowell Enterprises had just offered to keep her as a mistress in exchange for a condo and for "stuff" as he called it, even having the impudence to conclude "that's what girls like…"

But Chante didn't have the heart to put all the censure on the scoundrel. She was partly to blame too, remembering what happened between them in the bathroom of the suite where his mother was a patient.

"Shit…" she whispered between her tears.

But it was too late now for regrets. It happened and she had to live with it. In hindsight, she was confused why she even allowed it to come about. Had the patient, Samantha Lowell, or Nurse Betty, and Director Whittle come back and caught them in the illicit act, she would have lost her job as Certified Nursing Assistant, that's for sure.

It was with uncertainty that she reported for work the very next day. She had vowed the night before that she would refuse adamantly, beg even, not to be assigned to Suite 247 once again. But the floor seemed unusually quiet that morning. She learned that Samantha Lowell was discharged the night before. The private helicopter that brought her in brought her out, as well.

"Oh, thank God," was Chante's initial reaction.

She didn't have to suffer the awkwardness of seeing Jared again. Admittedly, she liked Mrs. Lowell. She felt a certain degree of kinship with the older woman. It made her a little sad, thinking she didn't get a chance to say goodbye.

But as the initial relief swept through her body, she was also assailed with a deep sense of melancholy. She won't be seeing Jared Lowell anymore. That, at least, was its own blessing, Chante thought.

The weeks that followed their departure, Chante often had to struggle with her feelings. She tried to focus on her work but often found herself looking out into space. She felt miserable, disconnected, and it took all her effort to keep going about her duty. The world lay heavily on her shoulders.

Nurse Betty took her aside and asked what was bothering her. Chante couldn't look her in the eye. The woman was very perceptive.

"Is this about a man?" Nurse Betty inquired.

Chante nodded her head. The supervisor didn't have to know who. So Chante decided on a half-lie.

"Yes…but it's over now…" Chante answered.

"That's good. If it didn't last too long, then he must be the wrong guy for you. Get out of that hole you crawled into. Someone better should come along for you." The supervisor consoled her.

Chante nodded her head in agreement. Nurse Betty didn't know how close to the truth she was. Jared

Lowell was definitely the wrong guy for her. It's about time she moved on and forgot all about him.

Things were slowly getting back to normal.

If you enjoyed this sample then look for **Love Astray: Audacious Billionaire BWWM Romance Series, Book 2**.

Other Books by Shyla Starr

- Persuasive Billionaire BWWM Romance Series

- Tenacious Billionaire BWWM Romance Series

- Elusive Billionaire Romance Series

- Lonely Billionaire Romance Series

- Fervent Billionaire BWWM Romance Series

- Audacious Billionaire BWWM Romance Series

Get the latest update on new releases from the author at:

https://shylastarr.com/newsletter/

About the Author - Shyla Starr

Shyla currently specializes in writing interracial romance stories and is a huge fan of the alpha male. Simply put, there just aren't enough stories about mixed couple romances, which is something she is aiming to fix.

Being a bookworm all her life, when Shyla discovered men she also realized how easy it was to fulfill her fantasies through her writing.

When not writing and fantasizing about men, Shyla enjoys dancing, reading and chilling with her friends.

Connect with Shyla Starr

I really appreciate you reading my book! Here are my social media coordinates:

Friend me on Facebook:
https://www.facebook.com/shylastarrauthor

Follow me on Twitter: https://twitter.com/shylstarr

Check me out on Goodreads:
https://www.goodreads.com/author/show/8436084.Shyl a_Starr

Subscribe to my newsletter:
https://shylastarr.com/newsletter/

Visit my website: https://shylastarr.com/

www.ingramcontent.com/pod-product-compliance
Lightning Source LLC
Chambersburg PA
CBHW031631200726
48288CB00019B/1374